FELIX POWELL, Boy Dog

FELIX POWELL,
Boy Dog

BY ERIN ENTRADA KELLY

GREENWILLOW BOOKS, *an Imprint of* HarperCollins*Publishers*

Felix Powell, Boy Dog

Text and illustrations copyright © 2024 by Erin Entrada Kelly

All rights reserved. No part of this book may be used or reproduced in any manner whatsoever without written permission except in the case of brief quotations embodied in critical articles and reviews. Printed in the United States of America. For information address HarperCollins Children's Books, a division of HarperCollins Publishers, 195 Broadway, New York, NY 10007.

harpercollinschildrens.com

The text of this book is set in Avenir LT Std.

Book design by Sylvie Le Floc'h

Library of Congress Cataloging-in-Publication Data

Names: Kelly, Erin Entrada, author.
Title: Felix Powell, boy dog / written and illustrated by Erin Entrada Kelly.
Description: First edition. | New York : Greenwillow Books, an Imprint of HarperCollins Publishers, 2024. | Audience: Ages 8-12. | Audience: Grades 2-3. | Summary: Animal communicator Felix's day takes a bizarre turn when a spell transforms the eight-year-old into a dog.
Identifiers: LCCN 2024004868 (print) | LCCN 2024004869 (ebook) | ISBN 9780063337169 (hardcover) | ISBN 9780063337183 (ebook)
Subjects: CYAC: Human-animal communication—Fiction. | Dogs—Fiction. | Magic—Fiction. | LCGFT: Animal fiction. | Fantasy fiction.
Classification: LCC PZ7.1.K45 Fe 2024 (print) | LCC PZ7.1.K45 (ebook) | DDC [Fic]—dc23
LC record available at https://lccn.loc.gov/2024004868
LC ebook record available at https://lccn.loc.gov/2024004869

24 25 26 27 28 LBC 5 4 3 2 1

First Edition

 Greenwillow Books

TO MAISIE
AND MARLOWE

C⊙NTENTS

1

THE BLANKET

You might think this is an ordinary blanket, but Felix Powell knows differently.

He discovered the blanket at Birdie's Thrift Shop, where his nan gave him five dollars to get anything he wanted.

Most eight-year-olds would walk straight to the toys, but Felix isn't most eight-year-olds. He went in the opposite direction. He explored.

The blanket was sitting on a haphazard stack of old quilts and comforters. No one had touched the blanket in fourteen days.

He unfolded it. He spread it out. He studied it from end to end.

It was blue.

There was a rip on one side, just big enough to poke a finger through.

Some of the threads were loose.

There was a patch where someone had mended it.

It was nothing special, to be honest.

But a little voice in Felix's head whispered: *There is something special about this blanket, Felix Powell.*

You should always pay attention to the little voice in your head.

Felix neatly folded the blanket, carried it to his nan, and said, "I'd like to use my five dollars to get this, please."

Nan raised her eyebrows. "It's summer in Louisiana and you have plenty of blankets. Why do you need this one?"

"Because," said Felix. That was the best he could do.

As it turned out, the blanket only cost one dollar. Felix went exploring again. He bought one yo-yo, two Amelia Bedelia books, and a charm bracelet for his nan. They were all fine purchases, but none of them were as special as the blanket.

That much he knew.

2

CATCH IT
WHILE YOU CAN

At home, Felix did research to uncover the mysteries of the blanket. "Active research" was something scientists did, and he wanted to be a scientist when he grew up. A wildlife biologist, to be exact. A primatologist, to be even more exact. That's a person who studies primates like chimpanzees and gorillas.

For now, though, Felix just wanted to find out what kind of magic lived in his blanket.

Because he was pretty sure some did.

Felix wore the blanket like a cape, hoping it would make him fly.

It didn't.

He sat on the blanket, hoping it would give him a lift.

It didn't.

He draped it over his head, hoping he would turn invisible.

He didn't.

When none of that worked, he tried something truly desperate.

He used the blanket as a blanket.

Still nothing happened.

"I have an excellent idea," said his dog, Mary Puppins.

Well, she didn't really *say* it, because Puppins only spoke Dog. To any other person, it sounded like this: "Ruff-woof-ruff-ruff-woof-bark." But Felix wasn't any other person, so he understood what Puppins meant.

"What's your excellent idea, Puppins?" Felix asked, as he sat cross-legged on the floor of his bedroom.

"It's a beautiful day," Puppins said. "Let's have a picnic in the backyard. We can pack meat loaf and roast beef and cheese and hamburgers and potato chips and cake and ice cream. And a banana."

Puppins was right about it being a beautiful day. Felix was certain he wouldn't be able to manage meat loaf and roast beef and cheese and hamburgers and potato chips and cake and ice cream and a banana on such short notice, but it *was* a glorious day for a picnic. The sun was bright. The sky was full of white, puffy clouds. And it wasn't too humid. When you get a day like that, you have to catch it while you can.

3

ULTIMATE NUMBER ONE FAVORITE SANDWICH

Food is important for any successful picnic, so Felix carried his blanket into the kitchen, tossed it across a chair, and made his ultimate number one favorite sandwich, which he called Felix's Ultimate Number One Favorite Sandwich. Puppins watched him the whole time. The kitchen was her favorite room in the house. She was intensely interested in what people did there, especially if it involved them accidentally dropping nibbles on the floor.

"Don't feed Puppins any of that sandwich!" Nan said from the living room.

Felix's hands were full—he had the sandwich in one hand, a reusable water bottle in the other, and the blanket across his arm—so he couldn't cross his fingers as he walked toward the sliding glass door.

He crossed his toes.

"And, Felix, remember we have our Bean Feast tonight, so don't get too full!"

Oh, yes! The Bean Feast! How could he forget? On the first Saturday of every month, Felix and Nan ate dessert for dinner. They called it their Bean Feast, even though there weren't any beans involved. Tonight they were having chocolate cake with raspberries and a side of ice cream.

"Okay!" he called over his shoulder, as Puppins walked at his heels, wagging her tail.

In the fenced yard, he spread the blanket on

FELIX'S ULTIMATE NUMBER ONE

INGREDIENTS

BREAD

banana

cinnamon

peanut butter

CRUNCHY

FAVORITE SANDWICH

INSTRUCTIONS

← bread

peanut butter →

banana slices ←

cinnamon ↑

← more peanut butter

→ more bread

the grass under the shade of the magnolia tree and ate his sandwich. The door on Nan's small garden shed creaked lazily nearby. Puppins sat next to him. Birds chirped all around.

Felix's backyard was small, but his neighborhood had plenty of trees, which meant it was busy with birds and squirrels.

Felix loved all animals, but his favorite was the bonobo. That's what he wanted to study when he grew up. Unfortunately, all the bonobos in the world lived in the Democratic Republic of the Congo, which was more than seven thousand miles away. Felix considered studying birds in the meantime, since there were plenty of them flying around. But they flitted by so fast, it was hard to tell them apart.

Felix loved listening to the birds. They all made different sounds, like *feeee-beeee* or *mew mew mew* or *ka-whee, ka-whee* or *caw caw caw*.

"Ka-whee! Ka-whee!" Felix said. He hadn't been able to communicate with any birds yet, but that didn't mean he wouldn't try. "Ka-whee! Ka-whee!" He stopped. Waited.

None of the birds responded.

Maybe one day they will, Felix thought.

Puppins liked to listen to the birds too. Well, usually. Right now, she was focused on only one thing: Felix's Ultimate Number One Favorite Sandwich.

He broke off a tiny piece of crust with peanut butter on it and gave it to her. She ate it without even chewing.

"I wish I knew how to fly an airplane," said Felix. He took a bite of his sandwich. "That way I could travel all over and see everything I want to see."

Not just the bonobos, either. There were hundreds of other things Felix wanted to see and just as many places he wanted to go. Sometimes Felix was overwhelmed with curiosities, like: What did animals dream about? Did mosquitoes have personalities? What did the jungle smell and look like? Would he be able to communicate with primates one day?

He could spend hours simply wondering about the mysteries of the universe. But he didn't feel like daydreaming today. He felt like doing something with his new blanket.

He finished his sandwich and took a big gulp of water.

"Now what should we do?" he asked Puppins.

Puppins drooled. "Make more sandwiches, then tear them into pieces and drop them on the ground?"

"I don't want to eat too much," Felix said. "Tonight is Bean Feast with Nan."

Puppins paused. "How come I'm never invited to Bean Feast?"

"Nan doesn't like to give you table food. You know that."

"Yes," Puppins replied sadly. "It's one of the greatest misfortunes of my life."

Puppins stretched out on the grass, thinking of her misfortunes, while Felix studied the fluttering of the magnolia leaves.

"How about we play hide-and-seek?" Felix

suggested. "I'll hide under the blanket and you seek me out."

"It's not much of a game if you tell me where you're hiding in advance."

"Okay, we'll call it something else." Felix twirled the curl of hair on his forehead, thinking. "We'll call it . . . Can You Free Felix from the Blanket While He Holds On as Tight as He Can?"

"It's a bit wordy," Puppins said. She stood up and wagged her tail. "But it'll do."

Felix got up and walked a few steps into the grass. Puppins did too. Then Felix dropped to his knees and slid underneath the blanket. He gripped the corners. He held on tight, tight with all his might.

"Try and get me!" Felix said.

Puppins didn't waste any time. She grabbed the blanket with her little teeth. She scratched it with her little paws. She barked at it with her

little barks. She tugged and tugged and tugged with the power of a Saint Bernard. A puppy Saint Bernard, but a Saint Bernard nonetheless.

Finally the blanket came off.

Puppins expected to see boy Felix, her best friend, with the curl on his forehead and a smattering of freckles on his cheeks.

But both Puppins and Felix were in for a big surprise.

THE BIG SURPRISE

Felix felt very strange. He could hear his nan taking a glass out of the kitchen cupboard, even though she was inside with the door closed. He could smell the apple core he'd tossed over the fence last week. His eyesight was funny too. Puppins's yellow fur didn't look yellow anymore. It looked gray. And the grass was gray too. Felix blinked.

"Puppins," Felix said. "What happened?"

"Hmm . . . ," Puppins said.

She trotted around him like an inspector.

"Hmm," she repeated, circling and circling. "Interesting. Verrrry interesting."

Then she did something truly odd. Well, it was odd to Felix. It wasn't odd at all to Puppins.

She sniffed his butt.

"Felix," she said. "You turned into a dog."

Felix laughed. Only it wasn't really a laugh. More like a crackled howl.

"That's funny, Puppins," he said. "It sounded like you said I turned into a dog."

"That's what I said."

"That's what you said?"

"Yes. Those were my *exact* words. 'You turned into a dog.'"

"'You turned into a dog'—those were your exact words?"

"*You* turned into a dog. I'm already a dog."

"So . . . I'm a dog."

"Yes."

Felix considered the likelihood of this and determined that it was highly unlikely.

"Very funny," he said. He scratched behind his ear using his back leg.

Wait—his back leg?

"Puppins!" Felix said, standing on all fours. "I'm a dog!"

"I know. That's what this whole conversation has been about."

"I'm not a boy anymore!"

"Not at this moment, no," Puppins said. "You're a mixture of both." She sat on her hind legs, puffed up her chest, and announced, "You're Felix Powell, Boy Dog!"

"Boy Dog!" Felix repeated. "But . . . how?"

"Maybe it was the sandwich," Puppins suggested.

"I don't think so. I eat that sandwich all the time. That's why it's the Ultimate Number One Favorite Sandwich."

"Maybe it was the water."

"Nan drinks more water than I do, and she hasn't turned into any animals that I know of."

Puppins looked around for clues, only to realize that there was a big clue right in front of her.

"It must be the blanket!" she said. She barked for good measure.

Felix looked down at his paws.

"But . . . ," he said. His heart pounded. He was suddenly aware of all the fur on his body. It felt . . . furry. Like he was wearing a light, cozy sweater. "But . . . ," he said again. He didn't know how to finish the sentence. "But . . ."

Puppins sniffed Felix from nose to tail while Felix stood very still. Well, that's not exactly true— he didn't stand still at all, because there were too many things capturing his attention. A leaf! A squirrel! A bird! A mosquito! A ladybug!

"Stand *still*," Puppins said. "I'm trying to sniff you out."

"I can't help it!" Felix said. "I see a leaf! And a squirrel! And a ladybug!"

Felix's tail wagged madly at the ladybug, though he didn't understand why. Sure, ladybugs were interesting and all, but they weren't something to get worked up about. Yet here he was, acting like the ladybug was an old friend he hadn't seen in ages. The ladybug crawled slowly up a long blade of grass. Felix pushed his nose toward it gently.

"Hello!" he said. "Ladybugs are supposed to

be good luck! Did you know that! My nan told me!
Is it true?"

He couldn't stop talking in exclamation marks.

The ladybug didn't acknowledge him, but it
didn't matter—Felix's tail wagged even *harder*,
smacking Puppins right across the face.

"Be careful with that thing," Puppins said.

"Sorry, Puppins! I can't help it!"

Puppins huffed then stepped back to observe
Felix in his full glory. "This is very exciting, Felix.
You're just like me."

"I'm just like you!" Felix repeated. He ran in
a circle. Then another circle. Then another circle.
Then another circle. Then another circle. Then
another circle. Then another circle. Then he
stopped with his tongue hanging out.

"Let's see if you can bark like me!" Puppins
said.

She barked.

Felix barked.

"Let's see if you can run like me!" Puppins said.

She zoomed across the yard.

Felix zoomed across the yard.

"Let's see if you can pick up sticks like me!" Puppins said.

She searched for a stick and snatched up a twig.

Felix searched for a stick and snatched up a twig.

"Let's see if you can dig holes like me!" Puppins said.

Puppins dug a hole.

Felix dug a hole.

"Let's see if you can rifle through smelly garbage like me!" Puppins said.

Puppins took off for the trash can.

BARK! BARK!
BARK!

Felix took off for the trash can . . . then he stopped in his tracks.

"Wait. What?" he said.

Before they could rifle through any garbage, however, something rustled in the magnolia tree. A leaf fluttered to the ground right in front of Felix's nose. He sniffed and thought: *feline*. He didn't know how he knew.

He just knew.

FELINE

Just as Felix suspected, a gray cat was slinking across a branch high above. It dipped its slender neck toward them.

"I found a ladybug!" Felix announced to the cat.

"Perhaps you should see if the dog boy can chase his own tail too," the cat said to Puppins. "Since that's the sort of small-brained thing you canines do."

"I prefer Boy Dog rather than Dog Boy!" Felix

noted cheerfully, his tail still wagging. "If you don't mind!"

"As a matter of fact, I *do* mind. I mind everything."

Felix recognized the cat. It was a stray that his nan liked to feed. She called the cat Madame Graytail.

"Trust me," the cat said now. "If you were going to turn into an animal, you could do *much* better than a dog."

Puppins huffed. "Go away! This is an A and B conversation, so you can C yourself out!"

Clearly, Madame Graytail wasn't the friendliest cat in the world. But Felix's tail wagged anyway. He didn't even think about it. It just *swish, swish, swished* like it had a mind of its own. He'd tried to communicate with Graytail before, but she had never talked back. Now he could hear her loud and clear. What other animals could he talk to?

"You don't have to leave! I love cats!" Felix said. "Plus, I know you. Nan puts out food for you sometimes. She calls you Madame Graytail."

"What a ridiculous name," the cat said. "I'm called nothing of the sort. Besides, my whole body is gray. Not just my tail."

Felix stopped wagging. He wanted to growl. Nan was excellent at naming things. She was the one who had named Puppins, after all.

"My nan doesn't invent ridiculous names," Felix said. "Only good names."

"Be that as it may," the cat said, sitting straight and tall. "My name isn't Madame Graytail. It's Gumbo the Magnificent."

"Oh please," Puppins said. "Your name is *not* Gumbo the Magnificent!"

Gumbo flicked her tail. "Okay, I added the magnificent part just now. But it's only fair. Cats are the most magnificent animals in the world."

"I think bonobos are," Felix said.

"I don't know what that is," Gumbo said. "But I'm sure they're far less interesting than cats. Name any animal, and I guarantee they are less interesting than cats."

"What about a rhinoceros?" Felix said. "Rhinoceros skin is up to two inches thick!"

Gumbo yawned. *"Bor-ing."*

"How about snails? Snails can sleep for up to three years!"

Gumbo slunk toward a lower branch. "Yawn."

Felix paused, thinking. "Whale sharks have around three thousand teeth!"

Bonobos are known for being intelligent, peaceful, playful, and creative.

Coyotes can be found in every state except Hawaii.

Skunks are immune to snake venom.

The black mask around raccoons' eyes help them see better at night.

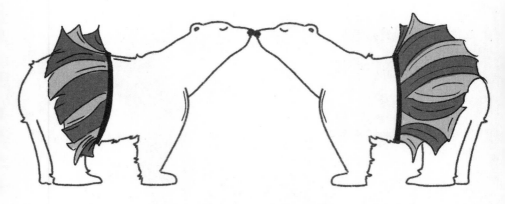

Sometimes polar bears communicate by touching noses.

"Please," Gumbo said, moving toward the end of the branch. "You're putting me to sleep."

Puppins leaned toward Felix and lowered her voice. "Trust me, this conversation will go nowhere." Her tail was *not* wagging. "Gumbo is a stubborn little show-off."

Gumbo jumped from the tree to the top of Nan's rickety old garden shed. Felix heard—clear as a bell—the quiet *clink* of Gumbo's claws hitting the tin roof. Then Gumbo leapt from the shed to

Beavers swim twice as fast as humans.

Octopuses have nine brains.

the grass. She moved elegantly, like a dancer.

"I heard that," said Gumbo. "Cats have excellent hearing. Better than dogs, even."

Puppins growled. "Not true!"

"It *is* true," Gumbo insisted.

"It is *not!*" Puppins said.

"My hearing is so advanced, I can hear everything happening in your brain right now." Gumbo leaned her head in Puppins's direction and pretended to listen. "It sounds like . . . complete and utter silence."

Puppins growled again. "What are you doing here, anyway? Shouldn't you be off grooming yourself somewhere?"

"Cats groom because we are very *clean* animals," Gumbo said. "Unlike some other animals I know." She sat on her hind legs and licked her front paw. "It's a shame you didn't shape-shift into a cat, Boy."

"My name is Felix," said Felix.

"Hmm. Your name is almost magical."

"What do you mean, almost?"

"*Feeee*-lix is almost like *fee-line*. Only it isn't. Unfortunately for you," said Gumbo. "Wouldn't you much rather be a *fee*-line, *Fee*-lix?"

"I like dogs *and* cats," Felix said. "And rhinoceroses and whale sharks and snails! But my favorite is the bonobo."

"So how did you manage to turn into a dog, of all things?" Gumbo asked.

"We're not sure," said Felix. "We think it might have something to do with my new blanket."

Gumbo raised her eyebrow at the blanket, which had been tossed into a heap after all the zooming and digging.

"Your *new* blanket?" Gumbo said. "That thing looks older than my grandmother."

"It's new to *me*," Felix said. "I bought it at Birdie's Thrift Shop, brought it home, crawled under it, and *poof*!" Felix spun in a single circle. "Boy Dog."

"This same thing happened to a friend of mine named Sally Sparrow," Gumbo said.

Felix's eyes widened. "You're friends with a sparrow?!"

"Befriend a *bird*? Ha! Don't be ridiculous. Sally is human, like you. She just happens to be named Sparrow. She turned into an animal too. Fortunately, she became a cat," Gumbo said.

"How?" Felix asked.

"She bought something from a shop. She put it on one day, and next thing you know . . ."

The sentence trailed off.

"Next thing you know, what?" said Felix.

"She turned into a cat. Like I said."

"That's the most ridiculous—and boring— story I've ever heard," Puppins said.

"It might have been boring, but it wasn't ridiculous," said Felix. "That's the same thing that happened to me!"

"Wait a minute, wait a minute," Gumbo held

up a paw as if to say *stop*. "The story was neither boring *nor* ridiculous."

"It was definitely boring. It had no details. No drama. You didn't even set the scene," Puppins said.

"I did so. I specifically said 'a shop.' And 'next thing you know.'"

"But something has to come after that," Felix said. "Stories are supposed to have a beginning, a middle, and an end. And there are usually sensory details. That means using the five senses—sight, smell, sound, touch, and taste—to describe things."

Felix thought about Mrs. Ruby, his favorite teacher at Getty Elementary School. She was the one who had taught them all about good storytelling.

"What do I know about telling stories?" Gumbo said. "I'm a ferocious street cat, not an owl."

"Ferocious," mumbled Puppins. "Puh-*lease.*"

Felix raised his eyebrows. "Do owls tell good stories?"

"Duh," Gumbo said, as if it was common knowledge.

"I thought you said cats were the most superior animals on the planet," Puppins said. "It sounds like you're not so superior after all. You can't even tell a decent story without boring us to death."

Gumbo sat up straight. "Cats are superior in *every way.* I'm sure that includes storytelling." She closed her eyes and raised her chin in the air like she was about to tell the greatest story ever told. Then she opened her eyes and said, "What did you say the story needed again?"

"Beginning, middle, and end," Felix said.

"With drama," Puppins added.

"And sensory details," added Felix.

Gumbo cleared her throat and began anew.

ONCE UPON A TIME THERE WAS A GIRL NAMED
SALLY SPARROW WHO WAS NOT A BIRD.

ONE DAY SHE DISCOVERED A SHOP. IT LOOKED OLD,
SMELLED LIKE SOCKS, SOUNDED QUIET, AND FELT
LIKE BRICKS. IT DIDN'T TASTE LIKE ANYTHING.

SHE WENT INSIDE AND SAW A RAINCOAT.

OH! AND THE RAINCOAT WAS GREEN WITH STRIPES AND OVERSIZED BUTTONS.

SHE PUT IT ON.

NEXT THING YOU KNOW

THE END.

A SUPERIOR STORY

"Well?" Gumbo said. "Was that not a superior story?"

Puppins let out a loud snore. "Sorry, were you saying something? I fell asleep."

"It was much better," Felix said. A bird landed on the fence post behind Gumbo. It was gray, just like the grass and Puppins. And Gumbo. "Is there an epilogue?"

Gumbo sighed. "What in the world is an epilogue?"

"It's the end after the end," Felix explained.

"There is no end after the end. That's why it's called The End."

"Sometimes things happen *after* the end. For example, did Sally remain a cat forever, or did she eventually turn back into a girl? And if she turned back into a girl, how did she do it?"

"Before I answer that, I have a question for *you*, dog boy," said Gumbo.

"Okay," Felix said, tail wagging.

"What day of the week is it?"

Felix paused. "Saturday."

Gumbo turned away. "Unfortunately, I don't give epilogues on Saturdays."

Felix's tail stopped wagging. "How are we going to find out if Sally turned back into a girl?"

"That sounds like a you problem," Gumbo replied.

"Oh, who cares about your dumb story!" Puppins said. "We don't need to know the epilogue because we don't care. Felix doesn't want to go back to being a boy. Right, Felix? Being a dog is so much better! People always think you're cute. You can run around all you want. You can dig holes and sniff garbage and get belly rubs and all the snuggles you want. Besides . . ." Puppins threw a mean look toward Gumbo. "Gumbo probably doesn't even know what the epilogue is."

"I do so!" Gumbo said. "Sadly, Sally turned back into a girl. She was happy about it, though I can't imagine why. Lucky for her that she didn't turn into a hole-digging canine who chased her own tail."

"I do *not* chase my own tail!" Puppins said. "That's a stereotype!"

"I haven't tried chasing my tail yet," Felix said.

"Give it time," replied Gumbo. Then she leapt onto the fence, effortlessly jumped into a magnolia tree, and disappeared.

LISTEN

After Gumbo left, Puppins turned to Felix and said, "Don't believe anything that fur-brained feline tells you, especially when it comes to sight and smell. Dogs are known for their extraordinary senses. Just listen."

Puppins turned an ear to the air.

Felix did too.

He heard a window open several houses away.

He heard the twitter of a distant bird.

He heard Nan put a glass in the sink. He heard her washing her hands. He heard her empty a puzzle onto the dining-room table. She liked to do puzzles on the weekends. Felix couldn't fathom why anyone would want to do a puzzle on such a beautiful day. Then again, he couldn't fathom why anyone would want to do a puzzle at all.

"If you concentrate and stand very, very quietly, you can hear so many unexpected things," Puppins said, her ears still perked at attention. "All you have to do is listen."

"I hear a crow," Felix said. "It must be blocks away! It's mixed in with other sounds, but if I concentrate, I can really hear it."

Puppins listened. "I don't hear a crow."

"Try concentrating really hard."

"I hear a car engine, lots of birds, and someone closing the lid on their trash can," Puppins said.

"I hear those things too. But I also hear a crow."

"Probably because of those big ears on top of your head. Dogs with big ears that stand up straight usually hear the best," Puppins said. "But not always. Golden retrievers have the best hearing of any dog breed. Their ears are big and really soft, but they hang down." Puppins gazed into the distance wistfully. "Oh, to be a golden retriever!"

"Why would you want to be a golden retriever?" Felix asked. Now that he knew he had good ears, he moved them this way and that. "I like you just as you are."

"Golden retrievers are the royalty of the dog world," Puppins said.

Golden retrievers are one of the most popular breeds in America because they are:
- friendly
- loyal
- playful
- affectionate
- smart

"What dog breed am I?" Felix asked.

Puppins looked him up and down.

"I have no idea," she said. "Maybe a Boston terrier mixed with a cocker spaniel mixed with a chihuahua mixed with a miniature pinscher."

"Is there anything about me that still looks like Felix?" Felix asked.

"You still have a curl on your head," Puppins said. Then she stood tall and asked, "What kind of dog breed am I?"

"I don't know," Felix said. Felix and Nan had picked Puppins from an animal rescue, so they weren't sure about her background. All they knew was that she'd been brought to the animal shelter as a puppy. "What do you think you are?"

"I like to imagine there's a golden retriever in there somewhere, with a dash of Saint Bernard," Puppins replied.

Puppins didn't look much like a golden retriever or a Saint Bernard, but Felix kept that to himself.

Puppins could be whatever she wanted, as far as Felix was concerned.

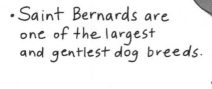

• Saint Bernards are one of the largest and gentlest dog breeds.

BUTT-SNIFFING, OLD FIGS, AND SWEETFACE

After a while, moving on four legs came easily to Felix. He walked naturally, like he'd been a dog his whole life. But there were many, *many* distractions.

Mostly smells.

Felix didn't just smell the grass or the dew or the garbage in the bin. He smelled the *bugs* on the grass. He smelled the *pollen* in the dew. He smelled the half-chewed chicken leg and the old coffee grounds and the banana peel in the bin. He smelled the rake and the lawn mower in the garden shed.

"It's hard to concentrate!" he said, his nose in the grass. "There are so many things all around!"

"Tell me about it. Dogs smell *way* better than humans. And way better than cats too. If me and Gumbo were in a sniffing contest, I would win, paws down. Too bad there aren't any bloodhounds around here. Then you'd really be amazed at what dogs can do," Puppins said. "Now that you're a dog, you have about a hundred million scent receptors, compared to just six million when you were a boy. That's just one way dogs are masterpieces of nature. We're not just great *hearers*. We're also great *smellers*."

"Wow," Felix said.

- Bloodhounds have about 230 million scent receptors— more than any other breed.
- They can track scents that are more than 12 days old.
- They also have the longest ears.

He wondered how many scent receptors primates had. He made a mental note to research it later.

"So," Puppins said. "Now that you know all about scent receptors, do you want to sniff my butt?" She turned around and lifted her tail.

"Ew!" Felix said. "No!"

"No need to be rude."

"Ew!" Felix said. "No thank you!"

"Butt-sniffing is a very important part of being a dog," Puppins said, looking back at him. "It's how we get all our information about each other, like whether you're a boy dog or a girl dog, the last thing you had to eat, and what kind of mood you're in."

"I'm a boy dog, the last thing I ate was Felix's Ultimate Number One Favorite Sandwich, and my mood is disgusted."

Puppins turned around so she was facing him again. "If you're going to be a dog, you'll have to sniff a butt."

"I won't be a dog forever," Felix said.

"Who knows? Maybe you will!" Puppins said. "Wouldn't that be fantastic?"

"Not if I have to sniff butts," Felix said.

"Instead of sniffing butts, how about we sniff something else?" Puppins's eyes brightened. "We could have a sniffing contest!"

"Okay," Felix said. He loved contests. "What are the rules?"

Puppins lifted her nose in the air. *Sniff, sniff, sniff.*

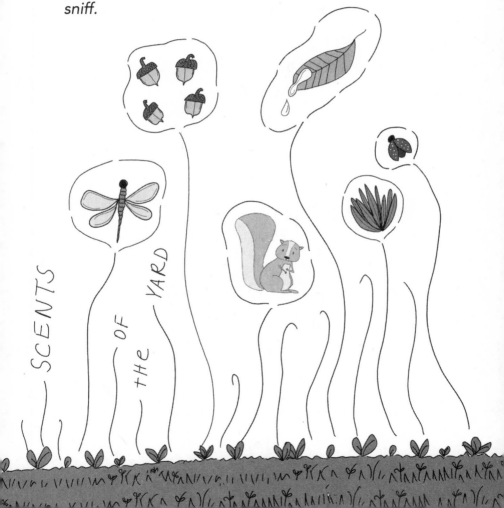

"I smell a fig," Puppins said. "Do you smell it?"

Felix lifted his nose in the air too. *Sniff, sniff, sniff.* Who knew the world had so many aromas? Grass, dewdrops, wet leaves, acorns, squirrels, pollen, car exhaust, dirt, bird poop. He had trouble separating one odor from another, but the more he sniffed, the more he concentrated. And once he concentrated—*really* concentrated, just like when he did math at school—the scent of a single fig sprang forward.

"Yes!" said Felix. "I smell it!"

"Let's see who can find it first," Puppins said. "Ready?"

Puppins reared back like a sprinter about to take off. Felix did too.

"Set?" Puppins said.

Their rear ends wiggled with anticipation.

"Go!"

Felix took off so fast, it felt like he'd left his dog body behind. But no, he was all in one piece, breeze blowing his ears back. He and Puppins raced to the corner of the yard. Felix's little black nose was wet and cool and gathered up all the fragrances. He worked madly through the grass. So did Puppins.

"Found it! Found it!" Felix yelled. If he were still a boy, he'd scrunch up his nose at the brown, shriveled fig, with all its squishy insides spilling out. But instead he was desperate to eat it, which he did.

"Where is it?" Puppins said, searching the ground at Felix's feet.

Felix's mouth was full. "It was right there, but I ate it." He swallowed. "I'm pretty sure I shouldn't have done that."

"How am I supposed to know you won if you ate the evidence?"

Felix opened his mouth wide and panted in Puppins's face. The smell of sour fig was unmistakable.

"Point taken," Puppins said. "You wanna race?"

"Okay!" Felix loved races. They raced all the time in gym class at school. Felix didn't always win, but he usually came in the top three.

Felix and Puppins lined up side by side near the shed. Puppins said "Go!" and they ran as fast as they could. Puppins won the first race. And the second. And the third. Puppins won all of the races, actually. Felix didn't mind. Puppins had a lot more experience running on four legs.

After her final victory, Puppins led Felix to the fence, which faced the sidewalk on their street. When they were done panting, Puppins said,

"Sometimes I stand here and wait for someone to walk by and tell me how cute I am. It doesn't take long."

"Do you think someone will tell *me* I'm cute?"

Puppins gave Felix a once-over. "Maybe," she said. "But you have to work on your sweetface."

"What is sweetface?" Felix asked.

"It's when you make your face as cute as possible. Like this."

"Why do you call it sweetface?"

"Because when people see it, they say, 'Look how sweet!' And then they scratch your ears and the top of your head and even your belly, if you let them. It's glorious." Puppins sighed. "You try."

Felix tried his own sweetface.

"We'll work on it," Puppins said.

They stood at the fence, looking out at the sidewalk, waiting. But the street was quiet today.

"What should we do now?" Felix asked.

Puppins tilted her head, thinking. They'd already zoomed around the yard. Dug holes. Run races. Picked up sticks. Had a sniffing contest. Half-sniffed butts. Tried sweetfacing.

Now what?

"Let's do some nice-thoughting," Puppins said.

"What's that?"

"My favorite activity of all," Puppins announced proudly. "All I need is a dirty sock."

NICE-THOUGHTING

Puppins trotted away, onto the patio. A dragonfly buzzed nearby. Felix could hear it *and* smell it, even if he wasn't exactly sure where it was.

Puppins sniffed one of Nan's outside slippers, said "This'll do," then picked it up and carried it over to Felix. The slipper was covered in dirt and who knows what else.

"Ew!" Felix said. "You're not going to make me eat that, are you?"

Puppins dropped the slipper at Felix's feet. "Of course not," she said. "I'm going to show you a popular dog activity. You'll like this one. Trust me."

Felix expected Puppins to lick the mud from the bottom or chew the dirt off the toe.

Instead, she curled up on the grass with her chin propped on the heel.

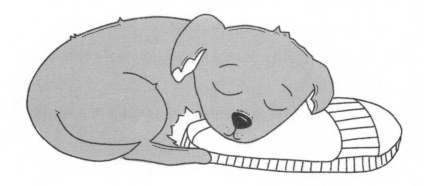

"There isn't an official name for this activity," Puppins said. "But I call it nice-thoughting."

"Nice-thoughting?" Felix repeated.

"Yes. It's when you lie around and think nice thoughts." She placed her chin on top of Nan's slipper. "It helps if you have something close by that triggers the nice thoughts, like an item that belongs to someone you love. That's why I steal your socks all the time. For nice-thoughting." Puppins closed her eyes.

Felix walked to the patio and picked up Nan's other slipper. It felt strange to have so many teeth, especially ones that were so sharp, but it made it easy to grab things.

He curled up next to Puppins with the slipper.

"What kinds of nice thoughts do you have with my socks?" Felix asked. "Do you think about the day we first saw each other at the shelter? Do you think about the first night you slept in my room?"

"Not exactly," Puppins said.

"Dog brains and boy brains don't work the same, so I can't really remember things like the day you picked me up or the first time I slept in your room," Puppins explained. "Instead, it's just . . . well, nice-thoughting. I associate one thing with another. For example, when I smell this slipper, I have nice thoughts about how much I love Nan and how she scratches my ears and how happy I am when she's around because she's my second-favorite person."

Felix didn't have to ask who Puppins's first-favorite person was.

"Try it," Puppins said. "You'll see."

So Felix did.

Nan's slipper

FAVORITE STORY

All the nice thoughts about Nan made Felix feel peaceful and content. They also made him feel a twinge of something else. Maybe a dash of sadness. He thought of her snapping the pieces of the puzzle together, then coming outside and wondering what had happened to him.

Mostly, though, he thought of how she brushed his hair after a bath. How they read

Amelia Bedelia together and they'd laugh and laugh. How she woke him up every morning with a sunshine song. (To be honest, sometimes he didn't like the sunshine song because he wasn't ready to wake up, but still.) He was just about to fall asleep with all these nice thoughts when Puppins said, "Felix, will you tell me a story?"

Felix yawned. It felt good to yawn—wide and open and drowsy. "What kind of story?" Felix asked.

He wasn't a great storyteller. Not like owls apparently were. At least he didn't think he was.

"Will you tell me about the day you picked me up from the shelter?" asked Puppins.

Puppins was still in the same spot, with her chin on the slipper. She looked extremely comfortable. To be honest, Felix was extremely comfortable too. The sun felt warm on his back.

The day Felix met Puppins was the best day of his life, and Felix wanted to tell the story in the best possible way. He decided to start with the setting so he could build atmosphere.

"It was a warm September day," he began. "Nan took me to the shelter right when it opened so we were the first ones there. . . ."

I WAS SO EXCITED, I DIDN'T SLEEP AT ALL THE NIGHT BEFORE.

This one!

She's a sweetie. And she doesn't have a name yet.

SUMMER BREEZE

Felix could have picked any dog at the shelter, but the little voice in his head told him he should adopt the yellow one with floppy ears, so that's what he did.

You should always listen to the little voice in your head.

Felix had a hard time choosing a name, but then his nan suggested Mary Puppins, and that sounded perfect to him.

"So we named you Mary Puppins," said Felix. "The end." He looked at Puppins. "Was that a good story?"

Puppins's tail wagged happily.

"It wasn't a good story. It was a *great* story," she said.

"Aren't you glad now that you're not a golden retriever? Because then someone else might have picked you before me and Nan even got there."

Felix smelled a ladybug and wondered if it was the same ladybug as before. Instead of pushing his nose into the grass, he lifted his head to the sky. He wondered what time it was. He heard the television in the living room, which meant Nan was done working on her puzzle.

"I guess it's good that I am who I am," Puppins said, closing her eyes contentedly.

"Definitely," Felix agreed.

Nan changed the channel. Felix could hear it.

Pretty soon, it'd be time for their Bean Feast.

Nan would come outside and call his name.

She'd see two dogs and no grandson.

He remembered a time last year when they got separated at the grocery store. Felix had wandered off to look at the cereal, and she hadn't noticed right away. When she found him, she hugged him so tight he could smell the laundry detergent in her shirt. The detergent was called Summer Breeze.

He could smell the detergent now too.

Felix looked at his paws.

"Puppins," Felix said. He felt the tickly grass against his belly and the warm sun against his back.

"Hmm?" Puppins said.

"I want to turn back into a boy."

TALL TAILS

Felix and Puppins thought the blanket would turn Felix back into a boy, but they were wrong. Felix crawled underneath the blanket just as he had earlier that afternoon, but when he emerged, he was still a dog.

"Now what?" Puppins asked.

Felix eyed the magnolia tree above them. "We need Gumbo. She can tell us the epilogue."

"That menace doesn't know a thing!"

"If she tells us the epilogue, we'll learn how Sally Sparrow turned back into a girl," Felix said.

"Why do you want to change back into a boy, anyway?" said Puppins. They trotted together to the center of the yard and faced each other. "Being a dog is marvelous. Everyone loves dogs! Didn't you have fun running around the yard? Didn't you love sweetfacing and nice-thoughting? Wasn't it fun to get your butt sniffed? And what about finding sticks and digging in the dirt?"

"Being a dog *is* really cool, but how will I have Bean Feast with my nan if I'm a dog?" Felix said. "How will I read books or study bonobos? How will I play kickball or ride my bicycle or make ultimate sandwiches or talk to friends or go to school?"

Actually, Felix didn't care so much about the going-to-school part.

"Maybe the first thing we should focus on is how to communicate with Nan, in case she recognizes you," Puppins said.

"How will she recognize me? I'm a dog!"

"You still have that curl in the middle of your forehead."

Was that enough? Could grandmas recognize grandsons by one simple curl?

"It's worth a try, at least," Puppins suggested.

"Okay," Felix said. He whimpered—just a little.

"We'll start with the tail, because that's the most important part of canine communication.

"You must know how to use your tail," Puppins continued, her voice very serious. "Most humans focus on the wag. But there are many ways to wag." She wagged her tail to further her point. "Repeat after me," Puppins said. *"There are many ways to wag."*

"There are many ways to wag," said Felix.

"Not all wags are the same," Puppins said.

"Not all wags are the same," repeated Felix.

"Dog tails are superior to cat tails."

"Dog tails are—"

Felix stopped. He heard—or at least he *thought* he heard—the quiet scritch of claws. Felix's ears twitched in that direction.

Puppins didn't seem to notice.

"Dog tails are superior to cat tails," Felix finished.

"Watch this," said Puppins. She swished her tail lazily back and forth. "This says, 'I'm relaxed and happy.'" She wagged her tail that way for a few more seconds, then suggested Felix try it.

He sniffed the air. Gumbo was back, he could tell.

Felix practiced wagging lazily.

"Good job!" said Puppins.

Without thinking about it, Felix's tail swished even faster. Something about hearing Puppins say, "Good job!" in a happy, cheerful voice made him want to wag with gusto.

"You're wagging now because you're *extra* happy," Puppins said. Her tail was wagging happily too. "Now let's discuss other modes of tail communication."

Before she could say anything else, however,
Gumbo jumped from the tree to the shed
to the ground. Felix had to admit
that she was
incredibly
graceful.

"Have you shown him how to chase his tail yet?" Gumbo said. She turned to Felix. "That's how small-brained dogs are—they smell derrieres and chase their own tails. Have you ever heard of cats doing such a thing?"

"I do *not* chase my tail!" Puppins said. "And derriere is just a fancy word for butt!"

"I would never say that word," said Gumbo, tipping her nose in the air. "It's beneath me."

"What word?" said Puppins.

"Butt."

"Hah!" said Puppins. "You *just* said it!"

Gumbo rolled her eyes. "Dogs. So immature."

"And besides, you and I *both* know that cats sniff each other's butts too!" Puppins said. "It's a completely natural greeting for cats *and* dogs!"

Gumbo paused. "Okay, fine. But it's not the *first* thing we do."

"Sometimes it is! You—"

"Listen," interrupted Felix. He took a step forward. "Can we stop talking about butts and move on to something more important?" He looked at Gumbo. "I would like to hear the epilogue of your story, if you don't mind?"

"As I said before, I *do* mind. I mind everything. And I don't discuss epilogues—"

"I know, I know. You don't discuss epilogues on Saturdays. But maybe you can make an exception this time so I can learn how to turn back into a boy."

"From the looks of things, you're learning how to be a *dog*." Gumbo's tail flicked. "Speaking of which, if you want to listen to tall tales about tall tails, you should learn all about how *cats* use theirs. Dogs aren't the only ones who—"

"I know, I know!" said Felix, exasperated.

"Look. Can we all just agree that cats and dogs are both great? *Please?*"

Gumbo looked at Puppins.

Puppins looked at Gumbo.

Gumbo and Puppins looked at Felix.

"No," they both said.

"Ugh!" Felix said. "Well, in *my* opinion—if anyone cares—you are both extraordinary animals, and right now you are both being extraordinarily annoying. Can we talk about Sally Sparrow? Please?"

"I'd rather not," said Gumbo. "I was thinking of taking a nap."

"Big surprise," mumbled Puppins. "Cats sleep, like, twenty hours a day."

"We do not!" Gumbo said. "Well, *I* don't, anyway. I only sleep sixteen hours and five minutes. And I've already lost approximately four minutes having this conversation."

WORLD'S SLEEPIEST ANIMALS

ZZZZZZ

KOALA: 20 HOURS

ZZZZZ

OPOSSUM: 18 HOURS

ZZZZZ

BROWN Bat: 19 HOURS

ZZZZZ

SLOTH: 20 HOURS

ZZZZZ

GIANT ARMADILLO: 18 HOURS

"How did Sally Sparrow turn back into a girl?" Felix said. "Can you just tell me really quickly? I don't want to miss Bean Feast with Nan."

Gumbo raised an eyebrow. "What in the world is a Bean Feast?"

"It's a special dinner I have with my grandmother once a month."

"Eating *beans*? Sounds more like a punishment."

"We don't eat beans," said Felix. "We eat desserts for dinner. We just call it a Bean Feast."

"Why would you call it a Bean Feast if you're not eating any beans?"

Felix sighed. "It's a term from Britain that Nan heard once. What difference does it make?"

"Who is Britain?" asked Gumbo.

"I wouldn't mind going to Bean Feast," Puppins noted. "Even if all we ate were beans."

BEAN FEAST OPTIONS!

ICE CREAM

PUDDING

STRAWBERRY SHORTCAKE

CHOCOLATE MOUSSE CAKE

FRUIT TART

"We're getting off topic!" Felix barked. "I need to know how Sally Sparrow turned back into a girl!"

Gumbo considered this. "It's valuable information, and I think I should get something in return for it."

"Isn't it enough to just help a friend?" said Felix.

"No," Gumbo said.

"See what I mean, Felix?" Puppins said. "This is why I don't make friends with cats. If *I* knew the secret, I would tell you right away."

"Ah, but you *don't* know the secret, so it matters not," said Gumbo, studying her paw like she'd just gotten a manicure. "Perhaps you should tell us more about tail communication, such as how you manage to run in circles when you're chasing it, or why some dogs don't know the difference between their tails and a chew toy."

"For the last time, I do *not* chase my tail!" said Puppins. "This is an X and Z conversation, so Y don't you leave!"

"I'll bring you cat toys!" Felix interjected. He thought he'd seen some at Birdie's Thrift Shop. Maybe he could convince his nan to go once he turned back into boy Felix. "And . . . and catnip!"

"Do you have these items with you right now?" Gumbo asked.

"Not exactly."

"Well, then it sounds like you have nothing to trade," said Gumbo.

Felix frantically looked around the yard for anything of value.

"I'll give you the blanket!" he said.

Gumbo turned away and began her slow, delicate walk to the fence.

"No thanks," she said. "If I sleep on that thing, I might wake up as a naked mole rat or a skunk." Over her shoulder, she added, "Or even worse—a dog!"

Puppins growled. "That's it! I've had it, you tree-climbing hairball!" She launched herself toward Gumbo, but Gumbo was much too fast—she effortlessly leapt onto the fence post, bounded to the shed roof, and jumped back onto her branch. She perched there, glaring at them, as Puppins barked and barked.

"If anyone needs me, I'll be up here taking a nap," Gumbo said triumphantly.

She stretched out, yawned wide, and tucked her head on her paws.

Felix could swear he heard her purring.

13

MR. MAGNIFICENT

"Gumbo isn't very nice," Felix whispered to Puppins. "Do all cats have attitude problems?"

"Some cats are very nice, even if they aren't as good as dogs," Puppins whispered back. "Gumbo happens to be particularly revolting."

"The only time I have an attitude problem is when I don't get enough sleep!" Gumbo called from above them. "It's impossible to get any rest with you two yapping about."

"This isn't even your yard!" Puppins said, looking up.

"All yards are my yards," said Gumbo. "The world is my yard!"

"Then can you go visit a yard on another continent, please?" Puppins said.

Felix looked up too and added, "Yeah! Like maybe in *Britain*!"

"I'm comfortable right here," said Gumbo.

"Don't you have mice you can chase? Or a hairball you need to eat?" said Puppins. A devilish look came over her face. "Or maybe you could visit Gregory."

Gumbo popped her head up. "What's that supposed to mean?"

Gregory was the very big German shepherd who lived a few blocks over.

"The owls told me you landed in Gregory's yard

the other day and he didn't take too kindly to you being there, even though the world is your yard," Puppins said. "They said you were so scared, all the hair on your back stood straight up!"

"That is a lie!" Gumbo said. But the look on her face told Felix that it was absolutely true. "Besides, why would I need to go into Gregory's yard when I can literally go *anywhere I want?*"

"I don't know," Puppins said. "You tell me."

"There isn't a single place that's off-limits to me," Gumbo said. She stood up and sprang from the branch to the roof of the shed. "Unlike dogs, I can fit into almost any space I please. Even tight little spaces like between the fence posts!"

She leapt off the shed and onto the grass, then hurried to the fence, where she slipped in and out of the posts without any trouble.

It *was* pretty impressive.

"Big deal," said Puppins.

"Yeah," Felix echoed. "Big deal."

Felix looked around the yard. He was tired of Gumbo. He really wanted to teach her a lesson, even though the little voice in the back of his head was telling him to leave it alone.

"I bet you couldn't fit in here," Felix said, trotting over to Nan's toolshed.

He stood in front of the door, which had a deadbolt on it. There was an eensy-weensy teeny-tiny sliver of space between one part of the door and the other.

"There's no way you would ever make it into the shed," Felix said. At that moment, he didn't feel like Felix Powell, Boy Dog, who wanted to swish his tail back and forth or talk to ladybugs or make friends or zoom through the yard. He

felt very much like a human boy with a grumpy mechanic in his body, turning his gears. If Gumbo was going to be thoughtless and selfish and mean, then he would be thoughtless and selfish and mean too. Let's see how she liked *that*. Let's see how it made *her* feel.

He wasn't sure what he wanted to happen, but he felt certain that Gumbo wouldn't be able to fit through the sliver in the door. Maybe she'd be embarrassed and have to admit that she wasn't right all the time. Or maybe she'd get stuck and he and Puppins could laugh at her until she cried. That would teach her a lesson.

Gumbo sauntered over and examined the shed door.

"I certainly *could* make it through there, if I chose to." She sat down. "But I don't want to muss up my fur."

Puppins stood next to Felix. "So you're saying you can't fit inside after all."

"I certainly *could*!" said Gumbo. "I choose not to."

"It's a forfeit, then," Felix said. That was a word he had learned from Coach Decker at school. He wasn't completely sure if he was using it correctly or not, but it sounded official.

"It most definitely is *not* a forfeit!" said Gumbo. She paused and glanced between them. "What is a forfeit?"

"It's when you can't play the game so the other team wins by default," Felix explained. "In this case, the other team is me and Puppins. The *dogs*. The *most magnificent creatures on the planet*."

Truthfully, Felix didn't think any single animal could be the most magnificent. All animals were interesting in their own way. But the mean gears were still grinding inside him, and he was convinced that the only way to make them go away was to make Gumbo feel sad or mad or bad or all of the above. He wanted her to feel just how *he* felt.

Gumbo raised an eyebrow at Felix. "Let's see *you* fit through there then, Mr. Magnificent!"

"I can't," Felix said matter-of-factly. "I'm a dog. My body is strong and wide." He put emphasis on the strong part. "Besides, I never said I could. I never said the world was *my* yard. I have my own yard. I have an *actual home*, right here with my nan, where I'm safe and warm *all the time*."

Felix couldn't be sure, but he thought he saw a change of expression on Gumbo's face—a quick flash of hurt in her eyes, so fast it was barely noticeable.

A little voice in Felix's head said, *That was cruel, Felix. You shouldn't be cruel.* A piece of him wanted to apologize right away, and he almost did. He even opened his mouth to say he was sorry, but different words came out instead.

"Just admit you're not as great as you think you are," he said. "And we'll all go on with our day."

After all, Gumbo didn't deserve an apology. *Gumbo* was the one who refused to help. *Gumbo* was the one who knew how he could turn back into a boy again. *Gumbo* was the mean cat. *Gumbo* was the bad friend. *Gumbo* was the show-off. Felix was the one who deserved an apology, not Gumbo.

Right?

14

CRASH AND CLANG

Gumbo crept
closer to
the shed
and peered
into
the opening.

"I'll fit in," Gumbo said. "No problem."

She stepped forward gingerly and wiggled her head through. Then the front of her body. Then the back. Her tail was the last to slip inside.

"I told you!" Gumbo said from the darkness. "I told you I could do it!"

Now Felix was *really* annoyed.

"Oh, who cares!" Felix said. He looked at Puppins. "Let's dig holes or play tug-of-war."

"I'll race you to find the best stick!" Puppins said.

They took off in different directions, noses pressed into the grass. Felix smelled a stick somewhere—at least he thought he did—but he couldn't find it. The grumpy gears were distracting him.

He hadn't been searching very long when a loud noise clanged from the shed.

Felix and Puppins stopped what they were doing and looked at each other.

"Did you hear that?" Puppins said.

"Gumbo's trying to bother us so we can't play tug-of-war," Felix said.

Clang!

Puppins barked once and said: "Gumbo, are you okay?"

"Something fell in front of the door!" Gumbo said. Her voice was muffled and trembling. "I can't get out, and it's dark!"

"You just want to annoy us!" Felix said.

"And who cares if it's dark?" Puppins added. "Cats have excellent eyesight in the dark, as you've reminded me a million times!"

"You're just upset because we don't want you to play with us!" Felix said.

But even as the words careened out of his mouth, he felt a tightness in his belly. He didn't quite believe what he was saying. Maybe it was his dog instincts. Maybe it was his boy instincts. He wasn't sure.

"Just because I can see in the dark doesn't mean it's not scary!" Gumbo said. "Please help! I'm afraid!"

The thing is, Felix didn't *want* to care if Gumbo was okay or not.

But he did anyway.

"Who cares!" Felix said. He turned around to face Puppins. "I bet there's nothing blocking the door at all."

But he knew Gumbo was telling the truth. He could tell by the sound of her voice.

Gumbo was trapped.

BARK!

BARK!

BARK!

OPPOSABLE THUMBS

Felix didn't know it was possible for cats to be afraid of the dark. In any other circumstance, he would have said so.

But this wasn't any other circumstance.

Felix and Puppins bounded to the shed door.

Felix pushed the door with his paws. He pushed and pushed and pushed, but the door didn't budge.

They heard another loud crash.

"Gumbo! Are you okay?" Felix said.

"Something else fell!" Gumbo said. She sounded truly terrified now.

"We need to unlock the deadbolt," Felix said. "Then we can open it and you can run out. I'll fetch the key!"

Felix took off, but he only made it three steps before he realized that he didn't know where the key was. He'd seen Nan unlock the shed dozens of times, but he had never paid attention to where she hid the key.

It could be anywhere.

"I don't know where it is!" Felix said. He ran to the patio and darted around frantically, looking for any hint of the key, but it was hard to tell what was what without bright colors to guide him.

"Use your nose, Felix!" Puppins said.

Felix hesitated. Yes, of course—he needed to search with his *nose*, not his eyes. "I found it!" he said. The metallic smell, mixed with the strawberry scent of his nan's hands, was unmistakable. He knocked over a plant, snatched the key that was under the pot with his teeth, zoomed over to Puppins, and dropped the key at her feet. They both looked at it. Then they looked at each other.

"Do you have the key? Do you have it?" Gumbo called.

"Yes, but . . ." Felix wagged his tail slowly.

"But what?" Gumbo said.

Puppins sighed. "We forgot something very important."

Felix's ears drooped. "Opposable thumbs."

ONE, TWO

There was only one way to get Gumbo out of the shed. That much was clear.

Nan had to unlock the door.

There was no other way.

And when she came outside, she'd find Puppins, one stray dog, one stray cat, and no Felix.

"If Nan finds you out here, she might take you to the shelter," Puppins said.

"I bet she won't," Felix said. "She'll probably adopt me."

That was what she had done before, after all.

Felix's mom couldn't take care of him anymore, so Nan adopted him.

She'd probably adopt him again—right?

Nan loved all creatures, boy and dog alike.

But that didn't make Felix feel much better.

"She'll wonder what happened to me," said Felix. "Boy Felix, I mean. She'll probably be really sad."

She would be. No doubt about it.

A bird moved in the nearby trees. Felix heard it. One of the neighbors opened and closed their front door. He heard that too. And maybe it was his imagination, but he thought he smelled Summer Breeze laundry detergent.

Maybe Nan would recognize him.

Maybe she'd figure it out.

Felix sighed.

No.

Not likely.

Gumbo paced inside the shed.

Felix heard it, of course.

"Gumbo, can you hear me?" Felix said.

He half expected her to say, "Yes, of course I can hear you. Cats have superior hearing, you know." But she simply said, "Yes."

"Puppins and I are going to bark as loud as we can until Nan comes outside," Felix said. "We'll lead her over to the shed and you meow really, really loudly. Then she'll hear you and let you out. Okay?"

Gumbo paused. "Okay."

"Ready, Puppins?" Felix said. "On the count of three."

"Ready," Puppins said, puffing up her chest to prepare for some super-high-decibel barking.

Just as Felix was about to say, "Three!" and launch into the biggest barking fit in the history of barking fits, Gumbo cried out.

"Wait! Wait!"

Felix and Puppins froze.

They stared at the shed door.

"Don't bark yet," Gumbo said, her voice quiet and soft. "I want to tell you the epilogue."

17

AN EPILOGUE ON SATURDAY

AFTER SALLY TURNED INTO A CAT, SHE DIDN'T KNOW WHAT TO DO.

I don't know what to do.

EVEN THOUGH SHE WAS A ✹ MAGNIFICENT ✹ BEAST, SHE WAS SCARED.

BUT SHE MISSED BEING A GIRL.

ONE DAY THE MOST BEAUTIFUL CREATURE
THAT EVER LIVED HAD AN IDEA.

OWLS ARE FAMOUSLY WISE.

THE OWLS SAID . . .

If you want to turn back into a human, the process is twofold.

One, an adult must say your name THREE times . . .

TWO—and this is <u>VERY</u> important—they can't touch you or you'll remain a cat FOREVER!

TWOFOLD

Felix's tail wagged. And wagged. And wagged.

"So that's it!" he said. "All we need to do is make Nan call my name three times in a row, and I'll turn back into a boy!"

Felix ran in a circle. Then another circle. Then another circle. Then another circle. Then another circle. Then another circle. Then another circle. Then another circle. Then he stopped with his tongue hanging out. "And she can't touch you," Gumbo noted.

"And she can't touch me," Felix said.

Puppins ran in a circle too. Then another circle. Then another circle. Then another circle. Then another circle. Then another circle. Then another circle. Then another circle. Then she stopped with her tongue hanging out.

"I'll bark until she comes out," Puppins said.

"I'll hide so she has to search for me," said Felix. He ran behind the shed and sat very, very still. He perked up his ears. He heard Nan inside the house. She was in the kitchen now, quietly humming "Home" from *The Wiz*, which was one of her favorite songs.

He leaned his nose toward the shed. He smelled Gumbo.

"Thank you, Gumbo," he said quietly.

Gumbo didn't say anything at first. Then she said, "You're welcome, Felix." She paused. "I'm sorry I didn't tell you earlier."

Felix wanted to say something else, but he didn't have a chance, because that was when Puppins started barking.

She barked with the might of a Saint Bernard.

She barked with the glory of a golden retriever.

She barked with the confidence of a teacup Chihuahua.

Soon enough, the back door slid open. Felix heard it, clear as a bell. He smelled strawberries and thread and apples and Summer Breeze.

Nan.

He had the urge to dart out of his hiding place and jump on her with his tail wagging fiercely. But he told himself to stay very still.

"Puppins!" said Nan. "What's with all the ruckus?"

Felix heard Nan step onto the patio, but he couldn't see anything from behind the shed.

"Where's Felix?" she said.

She stepped onto the grass. He heard it.

She walked over to the wadded-up blanket by the magnolia tree. She picked it up. She flicked it once, twice, three times, to get the grass off. Then she tossed it over her arm and went over to the overturned flowerpot. She set it upright.

Felix heard all those things too.

Please call my name, he thought.

His dog heart raced.

What if she searched the yard first and found him? She'd probably reach out to pet him. She'd probably swoop him up and carry him inside. And as soon as she touched him, he'd be trapped as a dog forever.

She walked to the fence and jiggled the gate to make sure it was locked. Then she put her hands on her hips and looked around.

If she came near him, he'd have to growl at her and bare his teeth. It was the only way he could think of to stop her from touching him.

But he didn't want to growl at Nan, and he hadn't even practiced growling and baring his teeth.

Felix moved farther into the shadow of the shed.

Nan stood still, looking around the yard.

Finally she called his name.

Felix had to stop his tail from wagging.

He waited.

Puppins waited.

Gumbo waited.

"Felix!" Nan called again.

Felix's heart went *thump thump thump.* He swallowed a big, nervous lump in his throat.

One more time, he thought.

But instead of calling his name again, Nan walked toward the shed.

The hair on Felix's back stood up.

She was only a few steps away now. Her shadow stretched across the grass.

She paused.

Felix closed his eyes and tried not to whimper.

Then: "FELIX!"

19

JUST FELIX

Felix emerged from behind the shed.

"Felix!" Nan said. She looked him over, head to toe. "Where were you? You scared me to death!"

"I . . . uh . . . ," Felix began. He felt so *tall*. He touched his face, just to be sure he was a boy.

"What have you been doing?"

"Uh." Felix shrugged. "There's a cat trapped in the shed. I was trying to help it get out."

"Why didn't you use the key?" Nan asked. She bent down and plucked it from the grass.

Felix didn't know what to say. He certainly couldn't say, "I turned into a dog and didn't have opposable thumbs."

Nan didn't wait for an answer. She unlocked the shed. "How did the key get all the way over here, anyway?"

"Be careful," said Felix. "I think some things fell over in there."

Puppins stood behind him, wagging her

tail and waiting. When Nan opened the door, a shovel almost fell on their heads. She caught it in midair and pushed it aside just as Gumbo burst out, meowing.

"Madame Graytail!" Nan said. "What were you up to in there?"

Felix looked at Gumbo and smiled. Gumbo meowed again, really loudly. As Nan locked the deadbolt, Gumbo rubbed against her legs, purring.

Nan laughed in surprise. "This cat never lets me touch her!" she said. She bent down and rubbed Gumbo's back. "I guess that's her way of saying thank you."

Puppins barked joyfully.

Felix bent down and scratched Puppins's ears. Then he scratched Gumbo's ears too. Just because.

"I guess so," he said.

"It's almost time for our Bean Feast, you know,"
Nan said. She pushed Felix's curl aside and kissed
him on his forehead. "Are you ready?"

"Yes," said Felix. "I'm ready."

EPILOGUE

(The End After the End)